To Alistair

For information address Hyperion Books for Children,
114 Fifth Avenue, New York, New York 10011-5690.
First Edition
10 9 8 7 6 5 4 3 2 1
Printed in Singapore
Reinforced binding
Library of Congress Cataloging-in-Publication Data on file.
0-7868-0958-2
Visit www.hyperionbooksforchildren.com

IT'S YOU, DADDY

John Wallace

HYPERION BOOKS FOR CHILDREN
NEW YORK

It was Little One's bedtime, but something was on her mind.

"Daddy," she said, "I have a question for you. . . ."

"Can you guess who my favorite person in the whole wide world is?"

"Gee! That's a tough one to answer," said Daddy.

"Give me a clue!"

"Well," said Little One . . .

"Who is **big**?
Who is STRONG?

"Who makes me laugh?
Can you guess?"

"This person sounds special," said Daddy.

"Give me some more clues!"

"Who is kind and gentle?" said Little One.

"Come on, Daddy, surely you can guess!"

"I'm trying," said Daddy.

"Oh, Daddy!" said Little One.

"Who can reach the top shelf
where the cookies are hidden?

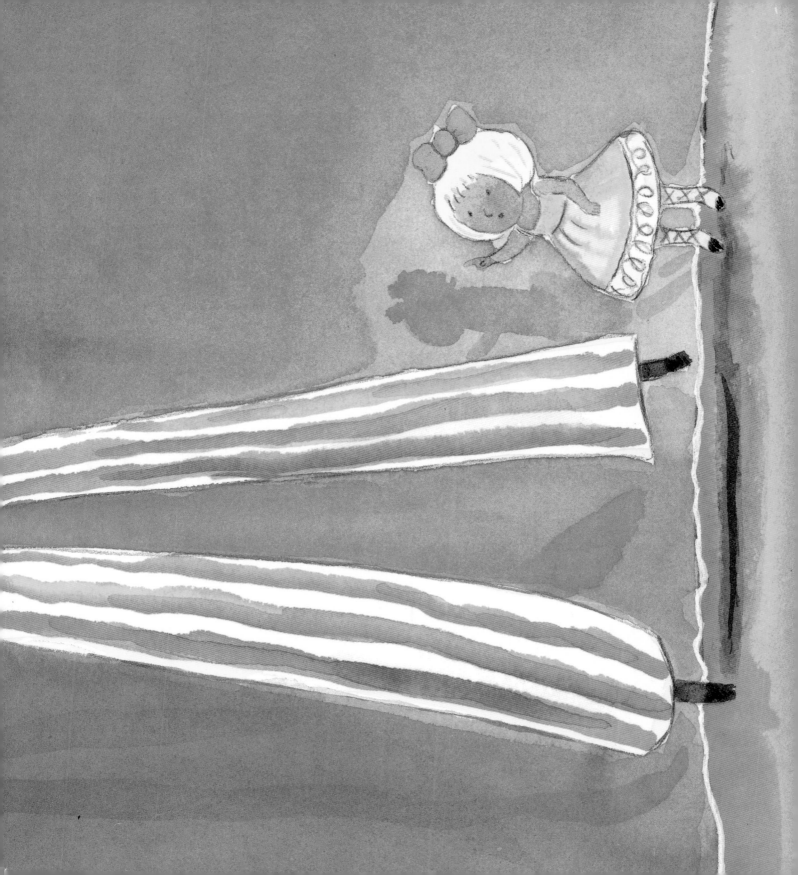

Who lets me dance on his toes?

"Who gives the best piggyback rides?

"Who swings me the highest?

"Daddy, who is everything to me?"

"I give up!" said Daddy. "Tell me who it is!"

"It's you, Daddy!
You're the best!"

Daddy smiled. He gave Little One a kiss.

He tucked her into bed.

"Good night, my Little One," he said.

"I think you're the best, too."

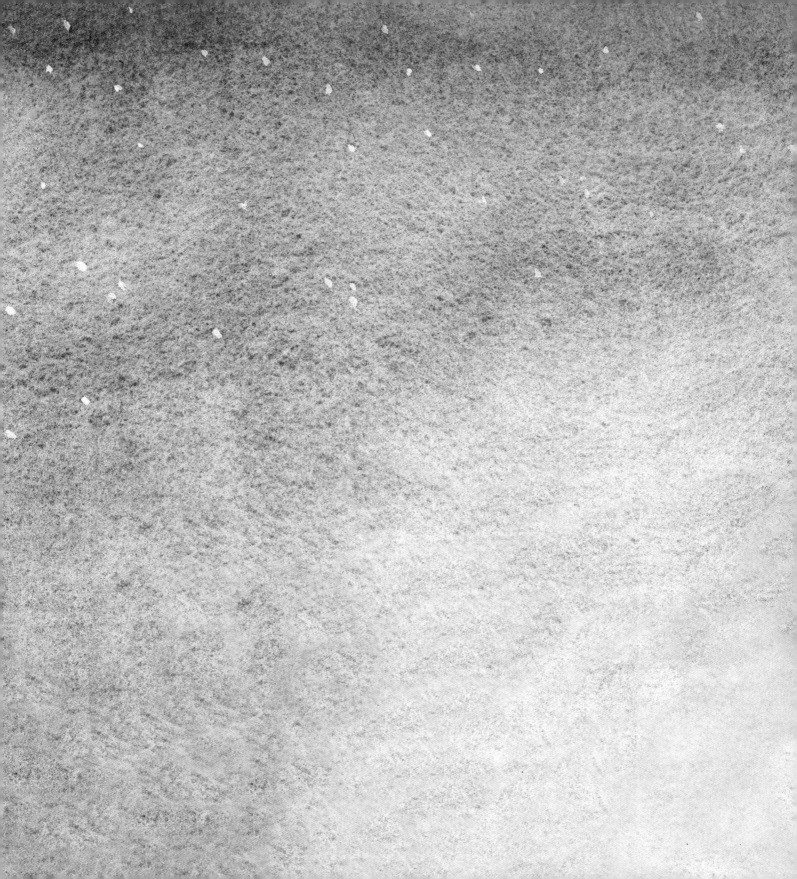